LITTLE PIG FIGWORT
CAN'T GET TO SLEEP

To the memory of Henrietta B and
to all sleepless piglets around the world.

C. M.

Clarion Books
a Houghton Mifflin Company imprint
215 Park Avenue South, New York, NY 10003
Text copyright © 2000 by Henrietta Branford
Illustrations copyright © 2000 by Claudio Muñoz

First published as *Little Pig Figwort* in Great Britain in 2000 by HarperCollins*Publishers* Ltd,
77-85 Fulham Palace Road, Hammersmith, London W6 8JB.

www.houghtonmifflinbooks.com

Printed in Hong Kong.

Library of Congress Cataloging-in-Publication Data

Branford, Henrietta, 1946-
Little Pig Figwort can't get to sleep / Henrietta Branford ; illustrated by Claudio Muñoz.
p. cm.
Summary: Little Pig Figwort cannot sleep, so he goes off to the North Pole,
the moon, and the bottom of the sea.
ISBN 0-618-15968-1
[1. Sleep—Fiction. 2. Bedtime—Fiction. 3. Pigs—Fiction.] I. Title.
PZ7.B737385 Li 2002
[E]—dc21   2001042093

10 9 8 7 6 5 4 3 2 1

LITTLE PIG FIGWORT CAN'T GET TO SLEEP

Henrietta Branford

illustrated by Claudio Muñoz

CLARION BOOKS · NEW YORK

Deep in a heap the little pigs sleep—Dill,
Chive and Caraway, Tansy and Pansy,
and smallest of allest, Pig Figwort.

"Sleep tight, little pigs," says Pig Mama.

"All night, little pigs," says Pig Papa.

Dill, Chive and Caraway, Tansy and Pansy
snuggled and snoozed, cozy and comfy and soon
deep asleep, sweet-dreaming the night away.

But little Pig Figwort could not get to sleep.

He opened one eye.

He opened the other eye.

He tossed and he turned,
he wriggled and he jiggled,

he tried and he tried,

but he could not get to sleep.

"I am a pig who likes to have fun," said little Pig Figwort.

"What I need is an adventure. What I need is a deep-sea dive in my submarine." Little Pig Figwort hopped out of bed.

He pulled on his deep-sea diving suit and squeezed into his submarine.

. . . he shot right down to the bottom of the sea, past an octopus sucking its thumbs, and a snoozing whale, past a sunken wreck, down to the bottom, where the mermaids race and the starfish shimmer.

"Ready, steady, go! Now for some fun!" shouted little Pig Figwort.

But the mermaids weren't racing, and the starfish weren't playing either.

"Shush, Pig Figwort," whispered a sleepy little mermaid. "Don't you know it's nighttime?"

She flicked her tail at him and tucked her seaweed blanket under her chin.

"Shush, little Pig Figwort," whispered
a starfish. "It's nighttime. Go home!"
   "Bother," said little Pig Figwort.
He squeezed into his submarine
and headed for home.

He snuggled down.
He shut one eye.

He shut the other eye.

He tossed and he turned,
he wriggled and he jiggled,

he tried and he tried,

but he could not get to sleep.

"The trouble is, I'm still not
sleepy," said little Pig Figwort.
"What I need is more adventure."

"What I need is a trip to the North Pole."
He snapped on his goggles and started
up his Ski-Doo.

"Ice and snow! Here I go!" shouted little Pig
Figwort, and he drove his Ski-Doo faster than fast . . .
up and over snow mountains and across glittering
glaciers to the far North Pole, where the polar bears
sled and the seals play hide-and-seek.

But the seals weren't hiding. They had all gone home to bed. And the polar bears weren't sledding. They were snoozing all in a heap.

DO NOT DISTURB

"Go 'way, Pig Figwort!" growled a big old bear. "Can't you see we're sleeping?"

"Bother," said little Pig Figwort.
He hopped back on his Ski-Doo
and drove all the way home.

He snuggled down.
He shut one eye.

He shut the other eye.

He tossed and he turned,
he wriggled and he jiggled,

he tried and he tried,
but he could not get to sleep.

"The trouble is, I'm just not sleepy
at all," sighed little Pig Figwort.

"What I need is something really,
truly exciting. What I need is a trip to . . .

. . . the **moon**."

He snapped on his space helmet
and climbed into his rocket.
"Five, four,
three, two,
one, **blast off!**"
shouted little Pig Figwort.

He shot over the treetops, higher than houses,
higher than airplanes, up to the moon, where
pigs fly high in the silver sky all night, because
it's much too shiny bright to sleep.

Little Pig Figwort flew with the moon pigs.

He looped the loop with them,

he ran races,

he played snoutball,

and tag, and hide-and-seek.

He played Pig Pirates,

Moon Jump,

and
Rocket
Races.

He played and he played
and when he just couldn't
play anymore, he tumbled
into his rocket and flew home.

"That was fun," said little Pig Figwort, back in bed.

"That was so much fun that I don't think I'll ever go to sleep again."

Little Pig Figwort shut one eye.

He shut the other eye.

He cuddled

and muddled

down into the heap . . .

Shhhh . . .

. . . little Pig Figwort is fast asleep.